Prilla's Prize

~• Book Seven •~

𝔇𝒾𝓈𝓃𝑒𝓎 PRESS
New York

Illustrated by the Disney Storybook Artists
Designed by Deborah Boone

Printed in China

First Edition
3 5 7 9 10 8 6 4

ISBN 978-1-4231-2922-6
T425-2382-5 12196

For more Disney Press fun,
visit www.disneybooks.com

"Oh, my!" Prilla cried as she raced toward a large field. "I'm late for Great Games Day!"

All the fairies in Pixie Hollow were getting ready for the games. The carpenter-talent fairies added last-minute touches to their go-carts; the animal-talent fairies led their birds through a complicated course; and the garden-talent fairies warmed up for the Potato Heft.

On Great Games Day, all the fairies got together to compete in exciting contests. The fairy who won first place in each game received a blue spider-silk ribbon.

More than anything Prilla wanted to win a blue ribbon. There was only one problem: she didn't know which contest to enter.

Every fairy in Pixie Hollow had a special, extraordinary talent. On Great Games Day, the fairies within each talent competed against each other. But Prilla was the only mainland-visiting clapping-talent fairy in all of Never Land. No other fairy had a talent like hers.

"What contest can I be in?" Prilla wondered aloud as she sat down on a toadstool.

Rani, a water-talent fairy, walked over. "Hi, Prilla!" she said. "Are you going to compete in the games?"

Prilla nodded. "Yes, but I don't know which one. You see, I'm the only fairy with my talent."

Rani smiled. "That's true. I suppose that means you could enter any contest you want," she told Prilla.

"You're right!" Prilla exclaimed.

"Hear ye, hear ye!" an announcing-talent fairy called. "The Potato Heft is about to begin! Whoever can lift the largest potato will win!"

"I can lift a potato!" Prilla said.

"You should try it," Rani told her. "Good luck!"

Prilla waved good-bye and flew over to join the gardening-talent fairies. She arrived just in time to see Lily lift a very large potato into the air. As Lily set the potato down, the other garden-talent fairies clapped.

Prilla walked over to the potato that Lily had lifted. She grabbed hold of its sides and fluttered her wings with all her might. But the potato wouldn't budge.

Next, Prilla tried to lift a medium-sized potato. But that was also too heavy.

In the end, Prilla could only lift a very tiny potato.

Next, the gardening-talent fairies lined up for the Carrot Toss. Whoever could throw a carrot the farthest would win. Prilla chose a baby carrot. Lifting it up, she threw it as hard as she could.

Plop.

Prilla's carrot landed two inches away. Beside her, a garden-talent fairy named Thistle hurled a giant carrot. It soared through the air, then landed in the dirt.

"Fifteen asparagus lengths!" the judge cried. "Thistle is the winner!"

"You gave it a good try, Prilla," Lily said. "After all, you've never had to lift a potato or throw a carrot before."

Prilla sighed. "But I didn't win a ribbon," she said.

Prilla flew back toward the main field. As she passed a stand of tall trees, Prilla caught sight of an obstacle course.

"This must be for the fast-flying-talent fairies," Prilla said to herself. She decided to take a look at the course.

"I see," she said, examining the obstacles. "Over and under the spiderwebs. Then hop in and out of the pots. Once around the pinecones. I think I can do it!"

"Prilla, darling, whatever are you doing here?" someone asked.

Turning, Prilla saw Vidia, the fastest of the fast-flying fairies. "I'm going to enter the obstacle race," she told Vidia.

"This race is for fast-flying fairies, dear," Vidia said with a sneer. "And you certainly aren't a fast flier."

"I can still try," Prilla said.

"Suit yourself." Vidia shrugged and went to the starting line.

Prilla's heart thumped as she lined up next to Vidia.

"On your marks!" the announcer shouted.

"Maybe Prilla should give us all a head start," Vidia said snidely. "After all, she is such a fast flier."

Prilla scowled. I hope I win this race, she thought. Vidia won't be able to make any nasty comments then!

"Get set," the announcer called. He blew on a reed whistle.

Prilla sprang into the air! But the fast-flying fairies were faster. As they soared forward, their powerful wings sent up a huge gust of wind, knocking Prilla back.

She tumbled down, down, down . . .

. . . and landed on the back of a frog!

With a loud *ribbit*, her frog leaped forward. Prilla grabbed the frog's neck and held on for dear life!

Looking around, Prilla realized that she was surrounded by animal-talent fairies. They were all riding frogs, too!

"Prilla!" Beck called. "I didn't know you were in the Leapfrog Race!"

"I'm not!" Prilla cried. "That is—not on purpose!"

Suddenly, Prilla's frog leaped off course.

"Not that way, Prilla!" Beck called. "The finish line is over here!"

Prilla tried to steer the frog straight. "No, silly frog!" she cried. "This way!"

But Prilla wasn't an animal-talent fairy. The frog didn't understand her.

Prilla's frog was in the mood for a swim. With a *splash*, it plopped into Havendish Stream!

"Prilla!" Rani said. "You're just in time."

Prilla looked up. Rani was kneeling on a leaf boat, peering over the side. She pulled Prilla aboard.

As Rani steered toward the bank of Havendish Stream, she asked, "Have you come to join the Leaf-Boat Race?"

Prilla looked around at the water talents. She still wanted to win a blue ribbon. "I didn't mean to join the boat race," Prilla admitted. "But now that I'm here, I'd love to try it."

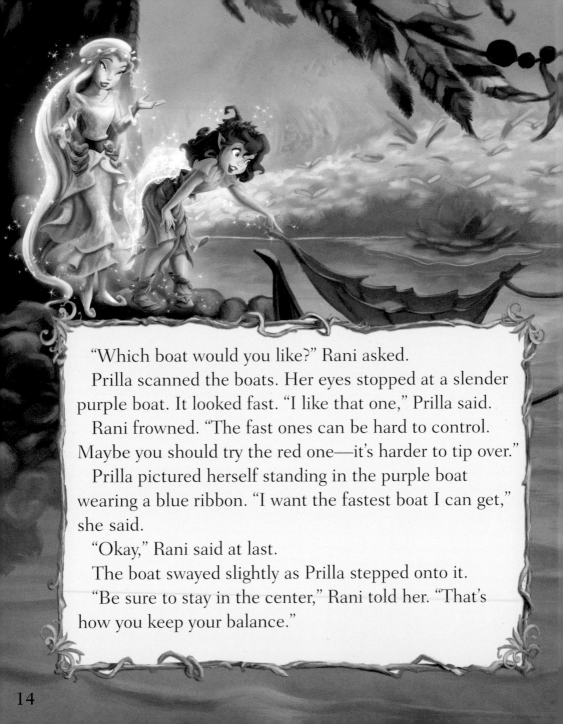

"Which boat would you like?" Rani asked.

Prilla scanned the boats. Her eyes stopped at a slender purple boat. It looked fast. "I like that one," Prilla said.

Rani frowned. "The fast ones can be hard to control. Maybe you should try the red one—it's harder to tip over."

Prilla pictured herself standing in the purple boat wearing a blue ribbon. "I want the fastest boat I can get," she said.

"Okay," Rani said at last.

The boat swayed slightly as Prilla stepped onto it.

"Be sure to stay in the center," Rani told her. "That's how you keep your balance."

The judge of the race rang a bell, and the boats took off.

Prilla dipped her paddle in the water. But her boat glided the wrong way. She tried paddling in the opposite direction. But the fast leaf boat zipped off course again.

"Come on, Prilla!" Rani called. "You can do it! Pull the paddle from front to back—not side to side."

Prilla plunged her paddle into the water and pulled as hard as she could. But the mighty pull was too much for the lightweight boat. It tipped, and Prilla felt herself falling overboard!

Luckily, a wave of water washed Prilla onto the bank. She was standing at the edge of a long green lawn, which was was dotted with pots and pans turned on their sides.

Clang! A dried pea rattled into a saucepan.

"Good shot, Tinker Bell!" called a fairy.

Smiling, Tinker Bell swung her ladle jauntily over her shoulder. Then, she caught sight of Prilla. "Prilla!" Tink cried. "What happened to you?"

Prilla blushed. "I fell into Havendish Stream," she explained. "Twice." Prilla told the pots-and-pans fairies about all the games she had tried.

"Well, why don't you try Ladle Croquet? You can borrow my ladle," Tink offered.

Taking Tink's ladle, Prilla aimed at a pea. Her whack sent it flying far into the woods. Prilla hurried after it. She searched under mushrooms, peeked inside mouse holes, and peered between roots. Finally, she found the pea in the middle of a patch of bluebells.

"I found it!" Prilla called as she raced back to the green lawn. But the game was already over.

Prilla sighed. It looked like she wasn't going to win a ribbon for Ladle Croquet either.

Prilla looked around the great lawn, wondering what other contests she could try. But it looked as if all of the games were already over.

A tiny tear trickled down Prilla's face. Now she'd never get a chance to win a blue ribbon.

"Prilla, what's wrong?" asked a soft voice.

Looking up, Prilla saw Rani and Tink. Each wore a blue spider-silk ribbon pinned to her dress.

"I entered so many contests," Prilla explained. "The Potato Heft, the Carrot Toss, the Fast-Flying Obstacle Race, the Leapfrog Race, the Leaf-Boat Race . . . I even tried Ladle Croquet. And I didn't win anything. I didn't even come close."

Rani turned to Tink and whispered in her ear. Tink turned to another fairy and whispered in her ear. Soon all of the fairies were whispering.

"What's going on?" Prilla asked.

"Prilla, everyone agrees that you've set a new record," Tink announced. She took off her ribbon and pinned it to Prilla's dress. "In honor of the most games ever tried, I present this ribbon to you, Prilla."

The fairies burst into applause.

Prilla blushed with pride. She had won after all.